Chapter 1

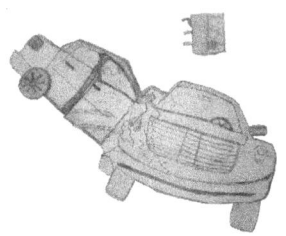

Changes

It was a beautiful day in the city — the skies were bluer than Becky had seen in a long time. Becky studied the sky while she and Jeff meandered through a quiet little park. Jeff pushed the baby carriage with Jake peacefully asleep inside.

All seemed perfect on this day.

As a flock of geese flew in formation overhead, Becky was reminded how she had always wanted to own a farm, complete with geese and ducks. She also knew that her husband's dream was to become fire chief. She and Jeff had been together since the ninth grade, and since then he talked about becoming a firefighter, and eventually chief.

As Jeff and Becky sat by a creek, Jeff noticed smoke in the sky. Seconds later, his fire pager went off. Becky looked at him and smiled, and said "go." He kissed her and Jake, and he was off. "Please bring home some milk tonight," Becky said as Jeff ran off. He turned and gave her a quick grin and nod.

That night, Jeff came home dirty and tired from a long day of work as a firefighter. Jake was crying in the background.

"Did you remember to get the milk?" Becky asked.

"No honey, I am so sorry, I forgot."

She kissed him on the cheek and said, "It's OK. You watch Jake and I'll run out and get some. Dinner is on the stove and I'll be back soon. I love you."

Thirty minutes later Jeff's phone rang. It was his chief telling him to come to a bad accident. "What is going on?" Jeff asked.

The chief gave him the address and said, "Get down here now!" Jeff took Jake to a neighbor and headed out with thousands of thoughts going through his head. When he got to the scene, red and blue flashing lights filled the sky.

Jeff noticed that all eyes were on him as he opened the driver's door. One of his fire fighter's buddies, Robert Jackson, walked toward him, but there wasn't the normal sense of urgency.

And there was a look in his eyes that made Jeff uncomfortable.

"I am so sorry," Robert said, holding back the tears. "A car ran a red light and hit her."

The puzzled look on Jeff's face told Robert that Jeff hadn't yet processed what was happening.

"It's Becky, Jeff. She's gone."

Jeff fell to the ground sobbing.

The next two weeks were like a blur. People were in and out of Jeff and Jake's home before and after the funeral. Family and friends helped by taking care of Jake. Jeff sat around in a daze, not sure what he was going to do without Becky. They had been together for so long. As the weeks went by, people stopped coming by as often.

Jeff took some time off from work to take care of Jake and himself. One day Jeff was just sitting in the living room on the couch and Jake was playing on the floor. Jeff was just sitting there in a daze. Suddenly he heard glass breaking and Jake crying out for Mommy. Jeff ran over and picked Jake up and held him. Jake had pulled a picture of his mom off the table. As his dad held Jake, Jeff realized he needed to snap out the guilt and start taking care of Jake and himself like he knew Becky would want him to.

Chapter 2

Jeff's Heroic
Setback

Jeff and his son Jake struggled in the years after the accident. They moved around often, and Jeff still felt like the accident was his fault: she would not have been at that intersection had he remembered to stop for milk.

He worked hard raising Jake and moving up in the ranks at the firehouse also trying to get over the past. He and Jake spent a lot of time together making their bonds strong.

Jake, now 10, struggled at school because he was different than the other kids. Smart but not athletic, Jake got picked on by a lot of other kids. One day a boy twice his size tripped Jake at lunch. Rather than fight back Jake, covered in his own spilled spaghetti, looked at the bully and thought about how he would use his talent for crafting things to get back at the boy.

 The next day Jake took a quarter that he sanded, down real thin and pried the locker open with it. Then Jake filled a balloon with water. With a coat hanger and needle he hooked it up in the boy's locker. He hung the balloon then hooked one side of the hanger on the door and put the needle on the other side of the hanger. When the boy opened the locker the balloon popped, covering the bully with water. The teachers knew immediately that Jake had done this and expelled him.

Jake's new school was next to the middle school. The middle school football team would pick on him because of his size. After one very difficult day of pranks played on him, Jake decided to do something. He invented a type of glue that would dissolve in 24 hours, then snuck in the football locker room and put the glue in all the helmets so the players could not get them off for 24 hours. Parents of those students were not happy when their kids came home with their helmets stuck on their heads.

Jake had to change schools again.

Jake had learned the hard way that he could not get revenge on others just because they did something to him. Jake's father knew that the reason he did those things was because he was picked on, but that was no excuse. He punished Jake and taught him to respect everyone and if he had a conflict with someone just walk away with his head held high, knowing he was doing the right thing

Jeff's top priority was to take care of Jake and keep him safe. After a diligent search, Jeff found a school for gifted children. Jake knew by the end of the first day the he would fit in well there. After a couple of years at the new school Jake was maturing into a responsible young man.

The two lived in a nice apartment building in the city and Jeff was still working hard as a firefighter. He hired a neighbor, a nice elderly lady, to look out for Jake while he was at work.

One morning Jeff walked into the kitchen and saw a robot arm taking toast out of the toaster and another robot carrying his coffee to the table. He walked to Jake's room, knocked and opened the door, triggering a

Ball bearing, which rolled down a track and turned on a light.

"Jake it's time to get up," Jeff said with a laugh. "Your gadgets have breakfast ready. I need to walk you to school early today. I have a meeting to attend."

"Dad, I am 13 now! Why can't I walk myself to school?"

His dad gave him that look — that one he's come to know. Without another word, Jake finished getting ready for school. With the loss of his wife and seeing tragedy every day as a firefighter — along with the trouble Jake used to get into, Jeff was very protective of his only son. Jake had finally gotten used to it. Wishing his mom was here as well, Jake tried to understand his dad's feelings.

Jeff and Jake walked down the street to the school.

"Ms. Jones will be picking you up after school today and taking you home," Jeff told his son. "She will be right down the hall if you need anything before, I get home late tonight."

Jake lowered his shoulders. "Okay," he said with a sigh. A little frustrated, he gave his dad a hug and ran into the school.

Later in science class Jake and his lab partner were putting the finishing touches on their science fair project. It was a robot that would play catch. Jake threw a ball to the robot, and the robot caught it. When the robot tossed the ball back, it flew across the room right past the teacher's head. She looked up and smiled at Jake.

"I think you boys still have a few more adjustments to make," she said.

The shift was pretty quiet at Firehouse 19, where Jeff worked. But 90 minutes before the end of the shift the alarm went off. Jeff and the other firefighters ran to suit up. The bay doors opened, and the trucks rushed out. The call went out that an apartment complex was on fire. A second call came through that there was a rescue at the same apartment complex. Jeff's team arrived right behind the first truck and went into the building. Dispatch reported that someone was trapped on the sixth floor. The team made their way to the steps where they encountered billows of smoke and fire.

About halfway up, a wall collapsed and separated Jeff from his team. He continued to the 6th floor, yelling and hoping someone would answer. Finally, Jeff heard someone crying out. He kicked down the door and smoke started filling the apartment. Jeff called out, trying to follow the screams. As he arrived in the bedroom where he had heard someone yelling for help, he noticed trophies from beauty pageants and a black belt in karate, along with ribbons and pictures of a beautiful young lady. There were also pictures of a happy family on the wall. Smoke and flames filled the room as Jeff saw the young girl in the corner. He ran over and saw that she had a large cut on her face and was bleeding and crying. As soon as Jeff picked her up, an explosion sent them out the window. Continuing to protect her with his body, they flew through the window, falling six stories onto Jeff's back. Other than the deep cut on her face, she was not physically injured. Jeff, however, was rushed to the hospital in critical condition.

A few days passed, and Jake was sitting in the hospital room with his father when the doctor entered. The doctor started talking to Jeff about his condition and recommended that Jake leave the room.

"Jake is my son, and we stick together," Jeff said. "Go ahead."

"I am sorry to tell you that you are never going to walk again," the doctor said. "The injury to your spinal cord is too severe."

Through the next few months, Jake walked with Mrs. Jones to the hospital every day to visit his dad. Jake went to therapy with him and helped with his routine. This event had made their bond stronger.

When Jake went home at night, he would stay up late to get the house ready for when his dad would come home. He made gadgets all over the house to make it easier for his dad to do things.

Four long months later Jeff did come home. Jake pushed his dad into the house and Jeff was amazed when he saw all the work that Jake had done. Jake lowered tables and shelves, so his dad could reach what he needed from them. He made other gadgets all over the house.

The next day, City Hall would give Jeff a medal for his bravery and sacrifices, even though he was medically retired from the city fire department.

Hundreds gathered in front of City Hall to honor Jeff for his bravery in saving Tiffany Scarlet Henson, a young, up-and-coming model and beauty queen. She lost her family in the fire, and her face was badly scarred. They gave Jeff a medal with Jake and Tiffany by his side. Jeff tried to hold hands with Jake and Tiffany, but she pulled back and stepped into the shadows.

Most people did not know that Tiffany had dealt with loss before. Her biological mother left her at a church when she was a little girl. Tiffany dealt with lots of anger. Her adoptive family put her in karate to help control her anger. It helped her to put her life on track. She would never talk about her life when she was young. Losing her family for the second time was way too much for her.

Chapter 3

Moving Day

Back in the apartment, Jeff was in the kitchen cooking in a gadget that Jake made for him. The device is on a track, so Jeff can slide across the floor standing straight up in the kitchen then slide to the table to eat. Jeff was enjoying this as Jake walked into the kitchen, they both laughed as they sat down.

"Jake, we need to talk," Jeff said. "I know we had to move after your mom passed, and with me in this wheelchair I cannot work for a Louisville fire department. I was offered a job as fire chief in a small town called Willisburg, Kentucky. They had an older chief there who, retired. He had paperwork all out of order and' bills not paid. That fire department was audited by the state and ordered to get everything in order in six months. My old fire chief heard about this and helped me get that job to get that place back in order."

"What about my friends and school?" Jake asked. "I fit in here."

Jake slid his food away from him and stood up to turn his back and started to walk away.

"Jake, stop. I am just trying to do what's best for the family."

Jake turned and said, "I know, dad."

He walked to his room. His dad let him go, knowing that he had been through a lot and was a good kid. Jeff was sure that Jake would come around.

As they drove from the city, it was mostly quiet in the truck. Jeff tried to cheer Jake up by telling him about the house they were moving into. Knowing that Jake liked science and building gadgets, Jeff tried to change the mood in the truck.

"Hey Jake, this house was owned by an astronaut from NASA, he said. "He passed away a few years ago and the house has been vacant since." He had no family, so the bank had to put it up for auction as is. So, his old stuff was put in the garage.

Jake nodded. He thought that was pretty cool and started showing some interest.

As they pulled up with the moving truck behind them, Jeff went to tell the moving people where to put everything. Jake got out of the truck when he heard someone say, "Heads up"! As he turned his head and ducked, a newspaper went flying past him. A boy on a hover board flew up the driveway, stopping fast and sending gravel everywhere. "Sorry about that," he said.

"You have great reflexes. Are you the new owners?"

"Yes," Jake replied. "I hope you are not as crazy as the old man that used to live there," Shane said. "Once, he dug a big hole in his garage (pointing behind the garage); that's where that big hill came from. I think he was making a basement, but he kept to himself mostly. I am Shane, the local newspaper boy. Got to go! See you around."

Before Jake had the chance to say anything the boy took off. Jake shook his head and thought that boy was a little odd. He started to walk around the house and garage looking at everything. He opened the garage and it was jam-packed with box after box. Jake shut the garage and ran into the house to help his dad.

The next day Jake was working on a project in his room. "I am going to the fire station!" Jeff yelled. "Be back in a little while!" Jake started to answer, and then he realized that his dad had never left him alone before. That put a smile on his face.

"OK, Dad. See you soon" he said.

Jake needed a tool to finish what he was making. He went outside to the garage and tried to open the garage door, but it was stuck. He went around the garage and found a window that was slightly open. He climbed up and saw a lot of things behind the boxes, like old computers and some cool-looking gadgets. As he climbed through the window his Jacket got caught. He fell to a carpet on the floor in the garage and stayed there for a second. As he tried to get up, the floor started to give way and he fell into the basement, through a hole that the astronaut made in the floor. There was a ladder going down, the piece of wood and a carpet was hiding it. "Great, the first time my dad leaves me alone I get hurt!" he thought as he lay in pain. He stood up, brushed himself off and looked around in amazement. With the light coming down through the hole, he could see computers, a film projector and some kind of chair with cables and electronics hooked to it. He had never seen anything like it before. There was a huge table in the corner with plastic on it. He took the plastic off to see what was there, but it was too dark, so he went to find a light to turn on. The only switch in the room was on the floor next to the computers. When he bent down and turned it on, the computers started to come on, one by one. Jake stepped back in fear. He noticed a global map on the table and a scanner with red lights start to scan the map. He didn't know what was going on. The film projector came on and the old film started to roll. He stepped back again and started to watch the film. An old man came on and started to explain the letter he had in his hand and the film that he was making. He said the letter is for NASA, explaining his discovery and designs. He went on to say that on his last mission to space, the planet they explored was dry and dusty and showed no life. On the ground he saw a tiny little pebble, green in color, about the size of a quarter. Knowing this was going to be his last mission he wanted to keep it as a souvenir, so he did not log it, nor did he tell anyone at NASA about it.

As the astronaut was saying all of these things, Jake noticed the letter that the astronaut was talking about and holding in his hand was on the table next to him, covered with dust and dirt. Jake thought to himself that the astronaut must have never gotten the chance to send the letter or film to NASA. The astronaut went on to explain what he had discovered. "The pebble I found was not like any other rock. I kept it on my desk in my garage. One day while working on a project, I spilled a cup of water and just a drop fell onto the pebble. Within seconds the pebble started to change. It started to grow a brown crust around it. I put on gloves and picked a piece of it off of the pebble and put it under a microscope. I saw thousands of energy particles in that small piece of crust. I was amazed and have never seen anything like that before. I continued to do tests on it because I wanted to see how much energy it was creating. I went to stick it with an energy reader and what happened changed my thinking forever. The energy reader I had in my hand and the piece of crust just disappeared in front of my eyes. Then I noticed the exact place I took the piece of crust off was back on the pebble and my energy meter was back on the shelf where I kept it.

"After five years of testing and experiments I have learned to control the crust and have been able to send objects back in time for only 11 minutes from the present time. Objects sent longer in time come back disfigured. The energy matter cannot be stable longer than eleven minutes. I have created this chair to send objects back intime and get them back again."

Jake just stood there in shock and amazement. The film stopped and was flipping over and over. Jake turned the projector off. Starting to look over the basement more, he heard a noise upstairs. He turned the switch back off and climbed up the ladder. He put some pieces of wood over the hole and the carpet over it as well. He opened the garage from the inside and got back in the house just in time to clean up before his dad got home.

Thousands of ideas were going through his head about what he had just discovered.

Should I tell NASA? Should I keep it to myself? Should I tell my dad? What should I do? After he got cleaned up, he was lying on his bed daydreaming of the possibilities when his dad came into the house.

"Jake, I have dinner! It's your favorite: pizza!" He walked into the kitchen pretty fast. Jake was sitting there in a daze, thinking about what he just discovered.

His dad waved his hand over Jake's face.

"Hello! You're not eating very much. What did you do today?" "Um, not much," he replied, still not sure what to say.

As they were eating, the TV was on in the kitchen. The news is showing a house fire live. There were firemen in the house attempting a rescue.

"I wish firefighters could get to a fire, moments before the fire breaks out so they can get the people out before anyone gets hurt," Jeff commented. That gave Jake a great idea. He looked up at his dad and started to leave the table. "Where are you going Jake? You only ate one piece."

"I-I want to go get that old garage cleaned up before the trash people come tomorrow. Is that OK?" "Yes, sure," his dad said with a smile. Jake took off to the garage.

Chapter 4

The Adventure Begins

A week had gone by. Jake spent most of his time cleaning the basement under the garage. While he was cleaning and moving things around, he was also learning to use the computers in the basement. He also spent time reading the astronauts notes on the pebble and how the chair works with time travel.

It took Jake a couple of days to find the pebble. It was in a metal box buried in the ground. The chair had cables connected to the table with the world map on it. A glass dish was hooked to the chair with cables going into the dish. According to the Astronaut's instructions, put a drop of water on the pebble and wait for the crust to grow around the pebble. Then take a piece of the crust and put it inside the glass dish on the chair and put the top back on it. His instructions went on: type in the desired time and location on the computer. The red scanner will scan the map on the table to pinpoint where you want the chair to go.

Jake thinks he is ready and waits for his dad to leave for work. After his dad left, he went and set up a video camera in the back yard then pushed the record button. Then went to the garage with a soccer ball. He waited a few minutes to make sure he captures it on camera. He is going to try to send the ball back in time 11 minutes. He typed in the location of his back yard and hit enter on the computer. The lights start to flash in the garage. The red scanner started to go back and forth on the map and the magnifying glass on the map points to the direct spot that he had set on the computer. In a flash the chair and the ball are gone.

Jake waited 11 minutes. The ball and chair came back to the garage, to the same spot. Jake laughed as he jumped up and down in excitement. A curious kid, Jake thought he would try sending the ball back longer than 11 minutes just to see what would happen to the soccer ball. Right before he started to do this, he thought he heard something upstairs in the garage. For the last few weeks, Jake kept getting the feeling he was being watched. He went upstairs but did not see anything. He tried to send the soccer ball back 15 minutes in time. It went to the backyard like it did before, but when the ball came back to the garage after 15 minutes all the black spots on the soccer ball were together and all the white spots were together. So, Jake programmed it on the computer to never be gone more than 11 minutes. No matter what, the chair will come back at that time.

Jake retrieved the camera from the back yard and watched the video in fast forward and saw the chair and ball appear and disappear both times. Jake continued to do tests like this for a couple of weeks, to learn more about time travel. One night at dinner he asked his dad, "Could I have that old TV set in the closet in the hallway to watch TV in the garage?"

"Yeah, sure," his dad replied. "You are spending a lot of time in the garage. What are you doing in there?" "Just working on some gadgets," Jake said. "Don't catch the garage on fire," Jeff said with a grin. "It would look pretty bad for the fire chief's garage to go up in flames." "Dad, you know I would never do anything like that," Jake replied. That night Jake took the old TV to the garage. He grabbed a city map from the glove box in his dad's truck and put it on the table with the scanner. He set up the TV and put it on Channel 4 news. The next afternoon his dad went to work. As Jake was working in the basement, breaking news came on TV that there was smoke coming from a home at a location outside the city.

Jake heard the address on the television and hurried down the ladder to put it in the computer. He thought this was his time to do some good, so people will not get hurt like his dad did, trying to rescue someone. With the computers set for 11minutes back in time he hit enter and ran to the chair. With his heart beating fast and his body shaking he hung on tightly, not knowing what was going to happen. The light started to flash on the scanner and scanned the city map. In a flash, Jake and the chair were gone.

Jake had set the locator to put him in an alley near the home that is on fire. With his heart still beating fast and him a little confused he jumped out of the chair. He set his watch for 11minutes and ran out of the alley, where he saw the house that was on the news. He ran to the home and knocked on the door and yelled for someone to answer him. After a minute a man opened the door and then ran to the kitchen where there is food on fire on the stove. He put it out and came back to the door. "Thank you so much," the man said. "I fell asleep and you woke me up. You saved my life!"

With a big smile on his face Jake quickly headed back to the chair; he arrived with a minute to spare. He and the chair disappeared as fast as it appeared in the alley and he was back in the basement of the garage. He jumped out of the chair nervous and exhausted looking in a mirror making sure he came back in the shape he left. Later that night he watched the news and saw nothing about the fire. Jake was so happy he could not sleep at all that night.

He continued to go back in time as the news reports on fires in the city were broadcast.

Time after time he went and came back. He was even more proud each time he could help save lives. Since he only could go back 11 minutes at a time. He only could get to

fires in time if news helicopters report fires right away, while they were flying around town. Jake was thinking to himself that at the fires he did get to, he saved lives and that was good with him. Then the news started to report that there were some common themes to some of the fires that were happening in a certain area of the city. They believed it was arson. They were broadcasting this on the news when his dad came into the kitchen to start cooking dinner. The man on the news was mentioning another common theme to these fires was a young boy getting people out of their homes before the fire was too big. There was a theory that the boy might be involved in setting the fires because he seemed to know when the fire was going to happen. As soon as Jake heard this he jumped out of his chair and turned the TV off. Luckily his dad was too busy cooking dinner to hear what they were saying. This made Jake a little bit nervous about getting caught. He thought about how much trouble he could get into for not telling NASA about the astronaut's discovery.

A couple of days later, Jake went to the garage and down the ladder. He noticed the light was on. He thought he had turned the light off before he left the day before. Not thinking much about it, he turned on the TV and started to work on the computer.

Chapter 5

The Encounter

The breaking news alert went out on TV. A family was trapped in a second-story apartment building fire. Jake started to take off but paused when he saw welding glasses on a tank. He put them on his face, so he could not be recognized. Then he put the address in the computer and arrived in the alley behind the building. He then set his watch for 11 minutes and ran into the front of the building to the second floor. When he arrived, he heard yelling from an apartment door. He opened the door and saw that a bathroom down the hall had smoke pouring out of it. A mother and her kids were crying in panic. With Jake's quick thinking he grabbed a quilt off the back of a couch and ran into the bathroom. He noticed that the bathroom window had been broken out by a glass bottle, which now lay broken on the floor. He got the quilt wet and smothered the fire. With only two minutes left on his watch, he ran out before the family could say anything. With just one minute left, he ran to the back of building to get in the chair. Out of nowhere someone threw a trash can lid, hitting Jake in the head, knocking him out, inches from the chair. A young woman screaming in anger ran toward Jake with a metal pipe. Out of the shadows a young boy flipped over the chair and Jake, and knocked the young woman down. Then Jake's alarm on his watch went off. With Jake still knocked out, the boy dragged Jake to the chair just in time. He and Jake arrived back to the garage.

The young woman stood up in the alley. She looked around, wondering were the two boys had gone. She was angry because she was the one that had been setting the fires. She also knew that Jake had been stopping them.

Back in the garage Jake woke up. He opened his eyes and saw the boy.

"You are the paper boy!" Jake said.

"My friends call me Flip," he answered.

"What happened?" Jake asked.

"It seems like some woman was not too happy with you putting out that fire," Flip said. "She threw a trash can lid at your head." "Where did you come from?" Jake asked.

"I live in the house on top of the hill with the big fence around it."

Jake thought for a moment and then said, "You are the one who had been sneaking around here watching me, aren't you?"

"Good thing I was, or she would have gotten you and you would be stuck back in time," Flip said.

Flip is a skateboarder with a punk attitude and some street fighting skills.

"Thank you so much" Jake said. "How much do you know about this?"

"I know everything. I have been watching since you moved in." Jake was puzzled.

"How did you go back in time with me?" he asked. "I'd see when you are about to go and would hang on the back of the chair,"

Flip replied. "I've been on a few trips with you."

Jake got up and turned off the machines. Still a little bit dizzy, he asked Flip to help him up the ladder. "I am going to rest," Jake said, and Flip started to walk off. "Thank you again!" he yelled. "See you tomorrow!"

Flip turned and gave him thumbs up.

Meanwhile in the city, the young woman, Tiffany Scarlet Henson walked to the apartment where she once lived. She ripped through the caution tape and walked up the steps of the burnt building. Walking into her old bedroom she rummaged through the ashes. With black on her face, she grabbed what she was looking for. She stood up with a sword in her hand. It was the one she used for her karate competition. Walking into the bathroom, she looked at herself in the mirror and stared for a moment. Then she took a pair of scissors and cut eyeholes in her black headband. She covered her eyes with it.

Then, she screamed and broke the mirror with her sword.

The next day, Jake and Flip were looking at projects that Jake was working on. "Did you get a good look at the woman that hit me?" Jake asked. "Yes, a little bit," Flip said. "She was tall, blonde and nice looking, but she looked very angry." Jake looked a little puzzled. "Some things are really hard to do on these old computers," he commented. Flip smiled. "I think I can help with that." They walked through the woods up to Flip's house then went through a hole in the back of the fence. Jake looked around in amazement there was a huge skate park, a swimming pool and a four, car garage hooked to a mansion. "This is yours?" Jake asked. "Yes, my dad's" he answered. "Is he a bank robber?" Jake laughed. "No." Flip said laughing. "He is a computer programmer for a huge company. "Flip walked over to the skateboard ramp.

"Check this out," he said. "This is a new trick I am working on for the junior championship."

Flip is one of the best skateboarders in his age group in the Untied, States. He got to the top of the ramp, jumped on the skateboard and zoomed down. Then he went up the other side, in the air. He did a flip while holding onto the skateboard, then back onto the ramp. Jake was amazed at how awesome that was. "You should win with that trick!" he said. "Thanks."

He walked over to a garage and opened the door. There were hundreds of computers there. Seeing the big grin on Jake's face, Flip said, "These computers will never be used. They were extras in a building project that was finished two years ago." Jake and flip carried several down to Jake's garage.

"I've got to go," Flip said. "I'll be back in couple of days. I'm going to a skateboard competition." "OK. I am going to rebuild stuff here. See you then."

Chapter 6

The Standoff

A few days later, Flip returned to the basement of the garage. He was shocked at what he saw. "Hey Flip, welcome back," Jake said as he continued working.

"You have got a lot done since I've been gone," Flip said. "Have you slept?"

"Not much." "Where is the table for the map and the chair to go back in time?" Flip asked. Jake raised his head again from the computer. "We don't need it anymore."

Flip walked over to the computer that Jake was working on. Jake stood up. "This watch is what sends us back in time now," he said. "How does it know where we're going?" Flip asked. "It has a web maps feature," he replied making them both laugh. A table was cluttered with all kinds of other things that Jake was working on. Flip and Jake walked over to a computer with the web on. "Did that woman happen to have a scar on her face?" Jake asked. "Yes, I think she did," Flip said. Jake went to play a video off the web showing a young woman in a beauty contest doing her talent — karate. "Is that her?" Flip asked. "I believe it is," Jake said. "I know her. She is the one my dad saved from a fire." "I saw in the newspaper that after the fire she went crazy and dropped out of college and disappeared," Flip said. "I guess losing her family was too much for her." Breaking news came across the TV set. A fire on top of the roof of a building downtown with a word spelled out: "SCARLET."

Flip looked at Jake. "I think that message is for you, Time." "Time" is a new name that Flip gave to Jake. Time stood in the middle of the floor with a bag of gadgets and Flip grabbed his skateboard and covered his head with the hood of his sweatshirt. "Let's do it," Flip said, and off they went.

Flip and Time arrived at the building that was on fire. They got there before Scarlet even had a chance to start the fire. They arrived on the roof and ran down the fire escape. Scarlet was walking toward them in the alley. "How do you get here before I even set the fire?" she asked. "What do you have, a crystal ball?" Time and Flip looked at each other and laughed. As soon as they did, she pulled a sword and started running at them. Flip grabbed his skateboard. Time threw a hook with a cable on it to the fire escape and climbed up to it. Scarlet swung her sword at Flip. Flip blocked it with skateboard. Scarlet kicked him in the chest and he fell to the ground. Time swung on the cable and kicked Scarlet to the ground. Scarlet stood in front of Time. He grabbed her arm and she laughed and said, "What do you think you're going to do now?" Time took handcuffs out of his bag and hooked one on her arm and one on the fire escape. She turned and looked at Time. She reached for her sword and cut the handcuffs off. Time's eyes got big as she ran toward him with the sword Flip jumped in the way and blocked it with his skateboard. Flip hit her in the leg with the skateboard. Then she turned and kicked him in the head and knocked him down. Time grabbed her around the neck from the back and she flipped him over her head to the ground. Flip came up behind her and she flipped the sword behind her back, stabbing him in the stomach. She stood up and stepped away.

She saw what she had done. Time ran and grabbed Flip, he held him on the ground.

"No!" he cried. Scarlet stepped away. Flip was gone!

A teardrop fell from Time's eye onto his watch. That gave him an idea. Time set his watch to go back 11 minutes again. He had never tried to go back in time once he was already there, but he had to try. He went back to the minutes before they showed up. He hurried and took a cable out of his bag and hooked one end to a dumpster, then threw the other end over a light hanging off a building and caught it. Then with all his strength he pulled the dumpster up in the air next to the light. He then hooked that end on the ground in the alley with a trip switch on it. Then he covered it with old newspapers that were in the alley. Time looked over and saw himself and Flip climbing down the fire escape. Then Time went back to the present. Time and Flip were standing on the fire escape again as Scarlet started to walk down the alley.

"So, there you are!" she said. Then she tripped on the cable switch, triggering the cable on the light. That caused the cable to drop the dumpster to fall down on top of Scarlet, trapping her inside.

Flip turned to Time. "When did you set that?" he asked. And Time just smiled. He called the police and they left. The police came and found fire-starting supplies on Scarlet and connected her to the other fires and arrested her.

Time and Flip were back in the garage, with only one minute left on the watch.

"That was a lot easier than I thought it was going to be," said Flip. Time put his gadgets away and laughed. Flip climbed up the steps and said. "See you on the next adventure!"

Chapter 7

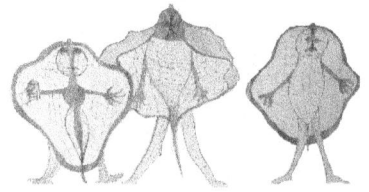

The Visitors

Hours later in the alley, three fish-looking aliens appeared with a special kind of scanner that showed flashes of green light where Time and Flip transported.

To be continued.

Author

Matthew Paul Landers

Editor

James Mulcahy

Editor

Terri Landers

Editor

Paula Pinkston

Editor

Austin Landers

Illustrator

April Williams

Illustrator

Melissa Williams

www.ingramcontent.com/pod-product-compliance
Lightning Source LLC
Chambersburg PA
CBHW071220130626
46555CB00004B/1784